The Knights' Wishing Well

A forgotten fairy tale.
By Michael "Fynn" Lange

To Jessie
Thanks for Reading
Michael "Fynn"
Lange

Dedication,

I would like to thank my family they have supported me every step I take. Second off I would like to thank my friends because when my family couldn't understand me they were there. Third I would love to thank all the people and places that have been a challenge to me, without someone or something to say no I cannot do that, or that I am a weird bizarre odd creature that they cannot comprehend, well without them there would be no adventure no stepping up and over. Without people like you there would be no stories. I give this forgotten fairytale to all who feel lost, to all who have thought at one point or another that they have to hide something inside of them that is beautiful and pure. I do hope you enjoy and remember, it does get better.

The Knights' Wishing Well

Once upon a time in a land less far far away than long long ago there was a dried up well, that as legend had it, would trade a wish for ones most valued trinket. This wishing well sat on the border between two of the king's most honored knights' land. Sir Caleb Hughes and Sir Warburton Kenly, this however is not their story. This is the story of their sons, which has long been forgotten, until now. This is a tale of their sons' adventures, their trials and tribulations and most of all their love.

The young Padraig Kenly with his jet black hair rushed through tall green corn stalks away from his family's farm. His face was rounded, with a strong jaw line that was already showing. He was nine years old. His entire life so far was about becoming a knight just like his father. The boy knew one thing, he was brave. Everything else he could figure out through that.

Padraig dropped a brown sack on the ground. He was a tad bit plump but had the potential to become a strong man. He leaned over the wishing well wall and looked down into the darkness.

"I wish..." he said bluntly, digging into his bag for a trinket. He let his fingers slip, dropping it down the well. Padraig whispered the rest of his wish as quietly as possible.

He sat down on the edge of the well after he finished wishing, crossed his arms and waited. Nothing was happening. He waited, and waited, very impatiently, huffing he grew agitated. He stood back

5

up to lean over the well. He looked down at the darkness of the well again.

"I said I wish..." and again he reached into the bag pulling out another trinket dropping it into the well. He whispered the rest of his words as gently as he could. He sat on the ground against the wall this time, twisting his leather boots around in the dirt and fiddling with his shirt sleeves. Waiting for what seemed to him like hours, still his wish was not fulfilled. He grabbed the bucket and rope from beside the well to set it up.

"You must not have heard me the first two times, do I have to come down there?" He said bravely. The boy put one foot in the bucket grabbed the sack and started to lower himself down into the well.
"I wish...," He attempted again as he lowered himself.
"I wish..." echoed his voice getting deeper down the well, then he hit the bottom. He twisted his head fast and hit it on the wall letting go of the sack and its contents.
"Ouch." The well echoed. He had wasted all his energy slowly lowering himself down the well, so when he tried to pull himself back up, he could not. His ego was bruised as his head grew a lump.
"Uhm, I think I change my wish. I wish..." He teased and whispered the rest of his new wish. Again nothing happened.
"Is it because I'm whispering? I wish to be out of this well." He demanded.
"I wish to be able to fly?" He questioned.
"I wish to go home, how about that, will that work?"

"Fine I give up I wish for help please, please someone help me... it is cold and dark down here. I hit my head, there's a bit of a lump growing." And fortunately enough for him another boy about his age was also approaching the well when he heard the wish for help.

"Is someone down there?" The new voice said.

"I am, can you please help me out?"

"Who is I am?"

"My name is Padraig."

"Hello Padraig, I'm Galloway. I am going to start pulling the rope up, do you have a foot in the bucket?"

"Yes Galloway."

And in a few minutes the boys met face to face. Galloway had eyes so blue they glowed and light blonde hair. His face was thin and long. Galloway was a half a year older than Padraig. Deep within his eyes you could tell within a few seconds that when it came to figuring out the way the world worked, he was already light years ahead of his new friend.

"That lump looks painful."

"It isn't so bad, it could have been worse."

"I think we have met before." Said Galloway.

"At court, your father is Sir Hughes."

"And yours is Sir Kenly."

"Yep that's my father bravest knight in the kingdom."

"Brave enough to climb down a wishing well?" Galloway gently mocked.

"Uhm yes but he would have been able to get out too."

"You got out with some help, you were very brave. How long were you down there for?"

"A few minutes, there are plenty of bugs down there and it's a bit moist, but you are right I was brave." Padraig smiled

"I was going to make a wish."

"I think this well is broken, we will have to find another one."

"Huh? Wait what did you wish for...?"

"It doesn't really matter it was something silly." Padraig said pushing his wish to the back of his mind.

"Alright but promise to tell me one day?" Galloway said.

"As long as I remember and you swear to be my friend and ally."

"Of course we will be knights together and roam the kingdom saving it from every foe we can."

"Deal." Padraig spit on his dirty rope worn hand and extended it to shake Galloway's. Galloway looked a little bit disgusted but did the same and they shook.

-

A half a year passed by like a lightning storm.

-

The boys had grown closer in the time that passed, almost inseparable. Their father's, Sir Warburton and Sir Caleb, began to take them to the castle. They were set to the task of playing hide and go seek with the king's daughter Yvonne. She was about five years younger than them. She had tight curly black hair so tight she could never get it into ponytails. The two would always be forced into losing as the princess knew the castle with all its nooks and crannies.

Galloway and Padraig had ruled out most of the castle for this game all they had left to search was the library. Padraig lifted chairs and moved aside tables as an out of place book caught Galloway's eye. He walked over sweeping his blonde hair out of his face. He felt the spine of the book as Padraig stood closely behind him. Galloway pushed the book fully onto the bookcase. Clicking noises could be heard from beyond the wall. Galloway jumped back as the bookcase swung open. Padraig caught him and stopped him from falling onto the ground. Cobwebs snapped as the void behind the bookcase grew.

Yvonne screamed, popping out from her hiding place. As she passed them they were both met with the coldest wind they had ever known, it was not after them however. She ran like lighting as the boys chased her keeping close. The frigid wind right behind the trio. Hallway after hallway, corridor after corridor she led them right to the king's throne room. Inside King Charlatte La Rue sat alone looking over some documents. As she ran for her father the gush of cold wind swept in slamming the doors of the room behind Padraig and Galloway. It was so icy cold they could see the blue crystals hanging in its surge. It picked her up for a brief minute holding her in its frigid arms then dropping her. Her mother's hairbrush came tumbling out of her dress and went skidding across the floor. She cried shivering as King Rue ran to her in terror. That was the last day they were to play with the princess.

To keep themselves from causing any more mischief they asked their father's to put them to work at the king's stables. This took up a good chunk of their day from then on out. They would work a hard day cleaning, tending to the horses as well as the riders that came and went.

-

Another few years passed as the boys became teenagers.

-

One day when their father's along with the rest of the knights were out, there was a fire in a hut near by the stables. Padraig, growing braver and stronger by the day rushed right into the hut as Galloway watched seemingly frozen for a minute. Galloway bolted for the town well yelling for help the whole way there. When he returned with other villagers and buckets of water Padraig was outside. He had saved the family of four.

Galloway led the bucket brigade to put out the smoldering smoking hut. In the end the hut was still standing, it had been saved along with the lives of two children, their mother and their great aunt. Galloway took a bucket over to Padraig and helped him wash his face off.

"You could have died you know." He said

"If I didn't do something they would have died."

"True, I didn't act very fast."

"You really helped though, I just rushed in, you went to get help. We make a good team."

"Yes I guess we do." Galloway said hesitant.

"I will see you tomorrow Galloway I need to go wash off, my mother will kill me if I show up all ashy to dinner." Padraig said walking away.

Galloway walked home on his own, thinking over the fire and how he should have acted faster, he should have been braver. The first thought he could think of is that he wanted to run away, that was his instinct.

"But Padraig rushed right in to save people's lives." This thought played in his head on repeat.

His father had come home that night in time for dinner. His mother placed hot soup in front of him and his father sat down nearby. They both looked at their son as they ate.

"I heard you and Padraig saved some lives and a house today. You will be knights in no time." Sir Caleb said.

"Father..."

"Yes Galloway?"

"How do I become brave?"

"You helped saved someone's house today, and their lives, you are brave."

"No I panicked and ran away, not like Padraig, he rushed right in and pulled the family out."

"Well we are each brave in our own way, and it is up to each person in which manner they will be brave."

"When did you discover your way to be brave?"

"When I met your mother I found my bravery, she was being held captive by a dragon. She inspired me in a way I had never been inspired. I tricked the dragon into a lake and tied a stone to its tail underwater so that it drowned. She still inspires me to be brave every single day of my life."

"How old were you?"

"Only a few years older than yourself, sixteen at oldest. Son do not fear you will find your bravery, you will find your strength I promise." Sir Caleb said, and Galloway went back to eating. His mind was thinking thousands of thoughts a second, which was pretty typical for him. These thoughts all focused on finding courage, finding his way to be brave. He finished eating and went up to his bedroom. He kneeled down by his window so that he could contemplate with the stars. There it was right in front of him, a way to find courage.

On the edge of his families land, on the opposite side of the wishing well away from the corn fields there was an old tower. Inside the old tower a wizard lived in solitude, Galloway had never seen him come or go, but he did know that the lamp in the tower's solitary window had been lit some nights and not others. His father had always asked him to stay away from the Wizard's tower, Galloway had never tried to push the topic. Tonight he felt he should do the opposite however. He rushed downstairs to find his father by the roaring fire place.

"Where are you off to at this time of night?"

"The tower."

"Galloway I have asked you to keep your distance the man inside asks not to be disturbed."

"He might be able to help me." Galloway puffed up his chest as much as he could.

"He might also punish you for offending the deal I made with him."

"Deal?"

"The wizard in that tower has lived there since long before I was born. When the king granted our family this land, tower and all, I approached the tower not to kick him out but to say that I knew the land was his. I would leave him be if he let me be."

"That sounds very just and fair, but I father am not you." Galloway was lowering his voice uncomfortably, he was trying to act like Padraig would.

"It will be your punishment then if he should decide to give you one."

"I understand." Galloway said and rushed for the door, practically jumping into his boots, then out like lightning.

"Be back before the fire goes out Galloway..." His father beckoned after him.

13

Galloway ran as fast as he could until he was within a stone's throw from the tower. He stopped on a dime almost falling over in the extra-large boots. He shivered in the brisk night air, the lamp in the window was glowing warmly way up above him. He would never be able to climb up, that was for sure. He paced around the tower seeing only hedges. Something was odd about the hedges, they grew thicker the closer he was, but if he took even a hair of a step back they retreated almost completely. By using this little trick as he walked around the tower he had found its doorway. He did not wish to enter unannounced he felt that might be pushing his luck.

"Excuse me Wizard my name is Galloway. I need your help with something, please."

"Go away boy only those of intelligence beyond your years can enter." A voice called back in a foreign accent. His syllables were short, each cut off rapidly as if the last letter didn't matter.

"My mother says I'm the most intelligent young man in the kingdom."

"All mother's say that sorry to tell you boy." The Wizard responded.

"If I can figure out how to enter your tower without any help will that prove my intelligence?" Galloway said pretty sure he had already came up with a solution in his head.

"If you enter I will assist you, good luck." The Wizard laughed, he was genuinely amused.

Galloway would leap forward and take a hair of a step back, the growth of vines was confused it grew, then retreated. Galloway repeated his little leap and shuffle step. Two more and if he wanted to he could reach his hand in, he was not sure yet how he should maneuver from here. Then something clicked. He

14

turned away from the entrance and jumped backwards in through the arch the hedges did not interrupt him. He dashed up the tower stairs to the room with the one window. The room was small. It had five walls even though the outside of the tower was round as round could be. A bed against rested with its left side against one wall, a desk against another. Books were stacked in piles all around the floor, while a cauldron sat unused. On the wall hung a map that depicted far away the islands of Manula and Lazan. There in a chair facing away from Galloway the Wizard scribed onto a piece of parchment.

"I have made it now you must assist me."

"I will keep my promise." The Wizard said. He stood from his chair, and turned to look at Galloway. The Wizard was not what Galloway had expected him to be. He looked like he was agelessly twenty years old, with caramel sun kissed skin, brown hair and almond shaped brown eyes so dark Galloway could fall in and get lost. His lips seemed almost purple, Galloway knew he was from a vastly distant land. He wore all silver and white robes, with a small rounded hat. A necklace that resembled clouds that changed shape as slowly as they would in the sky rested right under the curve in his collar bone. Galloway bowed immediately.

"Hello sir, again my name is Galloway Hughes. I require your assistance."
"So nice to meet you Gall. I hope you don't mind if I call you that. I am Doon Ay Nawala, call me Doon." The way the Wizard said his name was unlike any other name Galloway had ever heard, the d was separate and the o's came together like a French u. D' oon.

"Yes sir, I mean Doon." Galloway said as the wizard chuckled lightly.

"How may I assist you Gall?" Doon said. Galloway instantly liked the way Doon called him Gall. He felt comfortable, he felt he could do anything.

"I need to find courage, strength. I fear that I have none."

"I see. A young man on a mission, desperate enough to seek out a wizard that asked to be left alone. The young man might have been punished but now that he has shown a bit of cleverness will be rewarded. I will help you, if you never ask what courage is."

"Well how can that help?"

"I will teach you many things Gall but no one who ever asked for courage has been handed it. Courage and strength are earned. You shall earn them over time with my guidance."

"Agreed, I shall never ask, not even mention the word..." he did not say courage "I swear on my heart and soul."

"Good then, tomorrow night return here. Read this, as much of it as you can." Doon pulled a small blue book out from a shelf and handed it to Galloway. Galloway nodded and rushed down the stairs turning back once he was outside the tower to yell.

"Thank you Doon Ay Nawala." That night he would read the whole book without blinking an eye. His father stayed by Galloway's side at the fireplace watching the last ember die.

In the next few weeks Doon would give Galloway more books, scrolls and even a few works in other languages. Sometimes Galloway did not think he understood them. He would not let ignorance stop him, read them to the best of his abilities. When Doon would question him on them he would spout out the answers as if he had written the words himself.

As the moon beamed in through the tower window Galloway laid stomach down on the floor. His father's boots hung off his feet as he scribed out notes, Doon watching from his desk. Doon sometimes seemed to hesitate when he watched Galloway almost as if he did not want Galloway to catch him. This would of course make the clever boy curious so he would begin to ask Doon many endless questions.

"Padraig keeps questioning where I go most nights. Am I allowed to tell him?"

"That is up to you Gall. Do you feel he needs to know?"

"Not all the time, but sometimes he will give me this look and I will want to tell him every tiny detail about anything he asks."

"Sounds like you would even reveal that secret you have been trying to hide."

"What, no I don't have..." Galloway blushed. This was the first time anyone had called him out on the fact that he was somewhat different from the other boys. Much like Doon, he was in one way an outsider.

"Secrets are not a bad thing, we all have them. I have plenty myself. I want to tell you a small secret. Will you share it with anyone?"

"No sir." Galloway said eagerly almost jumping into the air. He knew no one would hear them, but still he crawled closer to Doon.

"Secrets build magic."

"My secret can make magic?"

"Have you ever been afraid of the dark so you light a fire, then the fire will die of its own accord?"

"A few times in the middle of winter and I am out of wood."

"In the darkness, when your fire has almost gone out all you have to do is to tell the fire your secret, if you are honest the fire will reignite."

Galloway thought of his secret. The last person he wanted knowing his secret right now would be Doon. Second would be Padraig, and currently those were the only two people that could come to mind. The torches on the walls of the tower grew stronger as he thought of his secret.

"Doon I don't want to be the only one like me."

"You are not the only one like you, not in that sense at least. I am like you Gall." The conversation ended there. That night Galloway slept in the tower on the floor, one of Doon's spare cloaks draped over him.

Galloway was beginning to understand something about himself that he hoped no one else would figure out. He thought it over in his head endlessly, the thoughts grew the more time he spent with Doon. He was alright thinking the way he did when Doon was around, Doon made him feel safe. However Doon never brought the subject of how they were alike ever again. If anything Galloway would almost have to drag it out of him, when push came to shove Galloway would withdraw with a simple, never mind.

-

Another few months flew by.

-

18

On the Kenly's land Padraig was riding one of his father's horses practicing his jousting when one of the other knights rode past him at full gallop. Padraig followed the knight back to the families' home. The knight knocked on the door and Sir Warburton answered.

"Sir Juniper what is wrong?"

"King La Rue has summoned all his knights to his side as soon as possible." Sir Juniper said as Padraig dismounted his horse. There was a very urgent manner at hand. Padraig's mother quickly gathered a bit of food as his father collected his armor taking the horse that Padraig had been riding.

"I will be back as soon as I can be." Sir Warburton said, kissing Lady Jane on the cheek.

"What is the problem?" Padraig said fast.

"Not this time boy, your father will tell you when he returns." Sir Juniper said.

"As always..." Padraig said and the two knights rode off. Padraig waited with his mother until the two knights were out of sight. Padraig took a step away from the house.

"Not this time Padraig," said his mother "Go find Galloway if your father's need you two then you will be ready." Padraig smiled and headed off to find Galloway.

A day passed by Sir Warburton and Sir Caleb did not return.

A few more days passed by, but no word had come about what the knight's had been sent off to do. The nights had grown longer, so much so that night had completely taken over the land.

Padraig woke up in what he thought was the middle of the night, but was actually supposed to be the morning.

"What time is it," He said as his mother looked out the kitchen window.

"It should be past breakfast, I wonder if your father is alright."

"I am not waiting anymore, I am going to fetch Galloway, and we will go to see the king."

Padraig was out the door, on a spare horse, galloping across the corn field and knocking at the Hughes's front door in no time. Galloway's mother Lady Claudia answered the door looking distraught. Padraig could see the pain in her eyes he could see the tears dried on her skin.

"Come in Padraig please, don't mind me I will fetch Galloway."

"No that is alright you have been through enough Lady Claudia, if you tell me where he is I can go get him myself."

"At the tower, he has been spending too much time with the wizard."

Padraig left his horse tied up by the house and ran to the tower where he met up with Galloway. Galloway was exiting the tower, the hedges filled in the space behind him.

"It's magic Padg." He said.

"The night time is from magic?" Responded Padraig.

"From who I do not know, I'm sure the king will know, I am also positive our fathers have gone to try and resolve whatever problem has caused it."

"Get a horse then we must rush off."

"My father took his, the others are not fit to ride."

"My horse can take two, hurry up." Padraig
said and the two hurried back to the house mounted the
horse, riding to see the king.

King Charlatte La Rue waited on his throne
while Yvonne stormed around behind him. She gave
them a bitter stare and stormed from the room servants
following after her.

"King Rue, please tell us what is happening."
Padraig said.

"I do not think you are old enough to help boys,
my knights have so forth failed at fixing this plague of
night."

"We are not our father's your majesty."

"That is understood,.." King La Rue paused and
thought. "This all started up in the valley of Kohln
where a dark warrior lives, Seff Jascquin. He cast
darkness and at first it was just over the small village.
When I sent your fathers up the darkness spread, and
kept spreading. Now as you know it envelops most of
our kingdom. He must be stopped but if my best
knights cannot do it I do not know who will."

"We will." said Padraig stepping up.

"You have no armor, nor horses how will you
stop Seff?"

"You can give us spare armor, I know our
fathers have some in the stables. The horses are easy as
well the kingdom has plenty. We will find our fathers
and stop this man."

"You boys could get hurt or worse."

"With no sun to shine on the crops people will
starve." Galloway said. The King knew he was right.

"Get them suited up." King Rue summoned to a
few servants. The two were taken to the stables and
given spare armor of their father's. The armor was far
too large, it would have to do for now. They were

given better horses and feed enough for three days' time. A messenger had arrived with two statues on the back of a cart. King Rue was out examining them in the court when the two knights walked their horses out.

"This is what he can do boys... this is Seff's magic." The two knights looked at the men, they knew them. They were fortunately not their fathers.

"We need to stop him."

"Go then young ones." The King said sending off Padraig and Galloway. The sound of breaking dishes could be heard from the castle they knew it was a tantrum of the young princess.

As they rode off toward the north east Padraig turned to Galloway.

"If we succeed... the King will make us knights for sure." Galloway sensed Padraig might have wanted to say something else. They rode on.

The farther they rode the darker the night became. Stars slowly stopped shining. Even the moon began to dim.

"It is too dark up ahead Padraig we will get lost."

"We must stop Seff." Padraig grunted.
"Hold back a bit, I have an idea." Galloway's studies were about to become handy. He dismounted his horse and searched the ground. He picked up an old dead branch, a stone and as much dried up weeds as he could. He began to make a fire. He tore off fabric that was hanging from the horse's saddle for decoration tying it around the top of the branch. Galloway lit it using the fire, he handed the torch to Padraig.

Galloway remounted his horse smiling proudly, the two began to ride again. As they progressed the fire as bright as it was seemed to dim, like the stars and moon before it. When it was almost a flicker the two stopped.

"Any more tricks Galloway?"

"You can't tell anyone though," Galloway said.

"Alright I won't, what are you going to do?"

"Promise me."

"I swear." As soon as Padraig swore Galloway took the torch pulled it close to his face and whispered some words as he waved his hand around the flame. The flame grew back to its original strength.

"You know magic? Why didn't you tell me you know magic?"

"It isn't something I like using."

"How did you do it?"

"It is a secret, please do not tell anyone."

"I swore, let's keep going." Padraig said. The two rode off once more. The fire did not dim again. Galloway's heart raced hoping Padraig would not question him farther.

Their path led them to a creepy sight. Many other knights had come out at the king's request. Most of them were now frozen in stone, their horses not too far away from them.

"Padraig this Seff is clearly dangerous."

"How do you figure he turns people to stone?"

"I am not sure yet, none of these men seem to be running, or aware of the situation at hand." They dismounted their horses. Both young men examined the knights further checking to see if their fathers were among them. Again they were not.

"Let's get going Galloway we have to stop this menace."

Once again the knights rode deeper into the darkness, their torch magically glowing brightly.

"The ground is covered in…words." Galloway said as he dismounted, playing with the mud at his feet. "The words are all negative. It is hate speech carved into the soil, against everything and anything." Galloway said reading the ground. Padraig dismounted his horse as well when suddenly they heard gasping and a deep voice not too far away. They crept towards the noise of the deep voice and came upon two knights, their fathers and a tall heavy set man dressed in all brown. It was Seff.

As Seff spoke his words came out as visibly dark smoke surrounding whoever he was speaking at. It made itself solid stone around the flesh of its victim isolating them.

"One who is not like I shall solidify." Vile words flowed forth from his lips as their armor began to turn to stone. "I cast you into stone for thinking you are being righteous. When you just hunt down the truly vigilant." He did not hear Galloway sneaking up behind him until Galloway was within arm's reach. Seff spun around grabbing Galloway by the arm and raising him into the air. His uncut nails digging into Galloway's armor, luckily his arm was so skinny he fell right out and delivered a swift kick to Seff's leg.

"Blinded by your own incorrect views are you boy?" Seff said and a darkness was cast over Galloway's eyes. Padraig in an effort to get in on the action tossed the torch and its flame caught onto Seff's clothing. Seff ran around magically burning until Padraig's sword met with Seff's knees. He dropped still on fire the heat and light making him suffer but not marked by a single burn.

"You have found me in the darkness, but I have also found the darkness in you boy." Seff said as Padraig chopped off his horrid head. Galloway quickly bagged his head. He approached his father.

"Mother misses you and she would like you to be able to come home. We will find a way to save you." He whispered into his father's stone ear. As he spoke the stone turned back to flesh. Once their fathers' were free the knights took their journey home. Along the way home they freed other knights in the same manor. By the time they reached the castle Galloway and Padraig had an entire army of knights behind them.

When they dropped Seff's head at King Rue's feet he smiled. Their father's and the rest of the knights stood around the grand hall proud to see these boys succeed.

"I proclaim both of you young men official knights." King Rue chanted as the knights cheered. Both of the boys were on one knee side by side, the backs of their hands touching. As the king's sword touched their shoulder they glanced at each other both feeling the same thought. It was too soon to try to communicate this shared bond, Padraig shook it off first, then Galloway.

A ball was held that night to honor all the dames, ladies, sirs and knights, those people the King Rue could call on whenever he needed. The castles main hall was decorated in purples and blues. Each families shield was raised high above the kings, suspended above the throne. Right at the center, the boar moon of the Hughes' and the noble stag of the Kenlys'. Lady Claudia and Lady Jane kept each other close company as their husbands were off telling tales they had both heard too many times. They looked over at their sons as the two women chatted they both saw what would happen one day.

"Do we tell them?" asked Lady Jane.

"Let them figure it out on their own." Said Lady Claudia.

"We could at least nudge them a little bit right?" asked Lady Jane. The two mothers each asked their son to dance, just once. In the middle of the dance, Padraig and Galloway found themselves suddenly facing each other hands clasped. Their eyes connected. The two boys laughed as if it had all been a good joke. Thankfully, to them at least, the music changed, the slow dance stopped. They both sighed relieved. The night went on without a single incident.

-

Years passed by as the two trained day and night, they began jousting and competing side by side as their fame grew in the kingdom.

-

On the night Galloway turned sixteen after he wished all his guests a safe trip home he snuck out his window in order to make his way to Doon's tower. Galloway approached the tower, the light was dim in the window. Galloway made his way inside as usual. Reaching the top of the stairs he noticed everything had been packed with the exception of Doon's pet magpie and a pile of opened letters.

"Dearest Doon,
We miss you dearly and wait till you can return to the islands. A love so far can not a family make. The Pack still trudge through the streets their awful rules will keep you away and we understand why but we wish it wasn't so.
Love Capit."

"Dearest Doon,
I heard from others, you are not the only one who was threatened to leave. One day return to me, one day when these ignorant men are gone. Please write back to me so I know how you are doing.
Love Capit."

"Dearest Doon,
There has been an uprising. Those of us who support magic are fighting back, we want our families united... please return and help us there are others with magic who have come back, I still love you and wish you to be at my side.
Love Capit."

Something in Galloway's heart changed. He felt stupid and unwanted, but he pushed it deep down he did not want to feel it, not here.

"Where is the wizard going Telulla." Galloway said a bit of anger and resent in his voice as he pet the bird, Telulla did not respond.

"Far Away." Doon appeared in the window.

"Hello Doon I didn't see you there." Galloway had grown used to Doon appearing and vanishing as he pleased. He had also grown comfortable with the fact that even though he was clearly growing up Doon never aged.

"Sorry I was busy arranging a few last minute details."

"You're leaving?"

"Yes."

"But, what about my courage, you swore you would help me."

"And I believe that I have, I have an extremely important matter to attend to Galloway I most likely will not return."

Galloway looked as if he might cry.

"I turned sixteen today Doon." Galloway said swallowing his words.

"Congratulations. Have you made a wish yet?"

"No I have not had one until now."

"Make it before your birthday ends."

"It is a secret."

"As wishes should be. My family needs me Galloway."

Galloway walked to the window and kneeled.

"I wish." Galloway paused, his wish had changed at least four times in the last few moments. He had to pick one. One was for Doon to stay, that was far too selfish somewhere Doon was loved. Then again Galloway thought he could be loved here. He wanted to wish this Capit another wizard, Doon was his. Then Galloway thought again Doon was Capit's first. The next thought was to be able to go wherever Doon went which led him to his final thought. What would Padraig do without him? Galloway made his wish.

"I know." Doon said as Galloway looked at him.

"Go on, you have a loved one that is waiting." Galloway said bravely understanding the final lesson. Doon vanished in a puff of smoke leaving behind a shield. The shield was emblazoned with Galloway's family crest, the boar moon. A new detail had been added as the same clouds as Doon's enchanted necklace shifted across the shield's face. Galloway slept alone in the tower that night. The shield was a gift Galloway would never let go of.

A half year passed slowly. The kingdom went without a single threat that needed knightly tending.

Then one of the worst threats came the Red Beast. The beast was made of raw red pulsating muscle, it would leave spoiled rotting land in its footsteps. This beast spread plague that was close to incurable and in the past those who has slain it had fallen down dead themselves not soon after. That fact however was not something that was said to the two young knights Padraig and Galloway as they rushed off as soon as the word came about that there was trouble.

The Red Beast had come up from the south and currently was ravaging the seaside town of Anama. Villagers lined the streets coughing and wheezing. The knights did their best to check if anyone had been bit or scratched, fortunately none had. They each did their best to point out where the beast had gone off to.

They found the Red Beast on the beach, where it had walked the sand had turned a spoiled green color, like open sores upon the shoreline. It twisted its head in unnatural ways. They drew their swords and raised their shields to protect the oncoming attack. They surrounded and fought it for half a day tiring it out. Eventually Padraig almost pinned tossed his sword to Galloway who plunged the sword right through the Red Beast.

The throbbing Red Beast was vanquished. As Galloway pulled out Padraig's sword a strange gas came out that Galloway breathed in.

"What was that?"

"I am not sure let's get this body to the King and go home."

They did just that receiving their praise and payment, which Galloway kept coughing through. When Galloway went to step down from the ceremony he passed out hitting the floor hard. Padraig carried him home after he was examined by the king's finest doctors.

Galloway grew more ill by the day. Nothing helped him, soon Padraig refused to leave his side. He would talk to him constantly begging him to awaken.

One night right before the sun was about to rise Padraig attempted yet again to talk Galloway back to health.

"Gall please wake up, please I need you." It was the first time Padraig had ever called him that.

"Doon you've come back..." Galloway said barely audible. His eyes closed, his hands gripped around Padraig's.

"It is me Padraig, I am the one who has been trying to heal you."

"No Padg would never know, he would never understand what is in my heart. He couldn't grasp my secret."

"What secret?" Padraig was sounding more agitated but would not leave the room now.

"I can't tell you then I won't be able to use it for magic."

"Secrets make magic?"

"You taught me that Doon stop being silly." Galloway responded. Padraig had never had much to keep inside, if he felt something he said it. So secrets had not been something he was used to but he felt a great secret growing inside. This secret held the two closest emotions one for Galloway and the other for Doon. So Padraig leaned down to Galloway's ear like he had once seen Galloway speak to a torch.

"I despise your Doon and I do not even know him. I," he whispered a four letter word "you." The words came out, they were a spell indeed. He had no idea why he hated Doon with the passion that he did, however his entire being was put into those fourteen words. The magic snuck in through Galloway's ear and began to do its work, Galloway continued to suffer in pain until he fully recovered two days later.

For those two days if Galloway was sleeping Padraig was there the second he would awaken Padraig would leave the room. When Galloway finally got out of bed Padraig left the Hughes house and went home. The first person he encountered was his mother.

"Padraig you look distraught, is Galloway alright?"

"He is recovered." Padraig said sharply.

"Are you alright?"

"I... something is changing about me, I think strange thoughts, I feel things I have never felt."

"You are growing up son. You are in the upswing of life. I think you may want to go off on your own for a little bit. Settle your head and your heart."

"I almost don't want to do anything."

"Then I request that you do have an adventure. My childhood friends sent me a letter about people going missing in their town, for me could you please go and see them."

"For you mother anything."

He put on his armor, then prepared his horse, mounted it and rode off.

He passed the castle of King Rue, after another few hours he passed through the valley of Koln. He was happy to see the small village had returned to its normal mountain lifestyle.

Then he went through a mountain pass and followed the road north until he came upon Timbre Town.

All of the buildings in the town were carved and built into massive redwood trees. As Padraig rode his horse through Timbre Town he began to notice all of its occupants were female. His mind wondered how Galloway might be feeling right now but he forced himself to put that aside. He was away to try and find out more about himself.

Padraig rode his horse up to the destination on the letter. Demona Dementia, and Ruby Lu Luscious spotted him from the porch. They stood up and walked down to him, greeting him at their gate. Both were very tall, at least two feet taller than Padraig. That would be without their extra five inches of high heels. He dismounted his horse and bowed his head.

"Hello there Ma'am, Ma'am. My name is Padraig my mother sent me to help you with something?"

"Yes we are your mother's childhood friends' Demona Dementia and Ruby Lu Luscious."

"My mother grew up among giants?"

"Not quite giants, but it isn't the worst thing we've been called." Ruby Lu chuckled.

"No matter your race, or lineage my mother has sent me to assist you so please tell me what you need?"

"Our youngest sister has lost her heart, the poor thing. Her name is Mamie Mistletoe. A heart is a horrible thing to lose. At first she just seemed to be in a daze but then after a day or two she started running away from home. She would run off in the middle of the night without her shoes on. She was brought back to us a day ago she began to speak latin, then after that she wandered off without her shoes towards the enchanted bookstore, we wouldn't dare go close. No one has come back from it since its last owner sold it."

"I am on it." Padraig said. Thus Sir Padraig got back on his horse, collected her blue glittery heels from the two giant like women and trotted off towards the enchanted bookstore.

His journey was fast for the road being steep. As he rode up the path he kept passing signs written in Latin.

"Si te, ne ante ullas catapultas ambules." said the first. He wished he had brought Galloway along instantly. He had barely listened when Galloway ranted on about learning the dead language. If he had ever listened he would know the sign read, *if I were you, I wouldn't walk in front of any catapults.*

"*Braccae tuae aperiuntur.*" *Your fly is open,* read another.

"*Sola lingua bona est lingua mortua.*" *The only good language is a dead language* read a third.

"*Non shirt, neque calceamenta, nullum servitium.*" *No shirt, no shoes, no service,* said the fourth. Finally he reached a weed ravaged yard and a rusted iron gate, a sign that hung over it read,

"*Cave ab homine unius libri.*" *Beware of anyone who has just one book,* it warned him but he could not understand it, so he dismounted forced open the gate and with his sword he cut a path in the weeds.

Padraig found his way to a small clearing with a water fountain, as well as a pedestal with a pair of silver stilettos. More script was engraved on the pedestal.

"*Tu pedes indutus, et antequam intres eundum quo nemo ante iit.*" *Before you may enter you must put on the heels and boldly go where no man has gone before.* Read the sign below the stilettos.

Beyond the pedestal and another jungle of weeds he found the porch and the locked front door. He could not get the door to budge a single inch. On his way back away from the building he accidentally tripped into the pedestal with the stilettos on it. The door began clicking and creaking. He now knew what he had to do, Padraig may not have been clever but he was not as dim as most seemed to think. He took off his boots, removed his thick socks and strapped on the heels.

He began his journey heels and all into the bookstore. The bookstore was once beautiful. Kingdoms' would send their best scholars to submit their works here. Everyone in the kingdom dreamed of this bookstore, even Galloway had spoken of its former glory. Within the last few years its owner changed hands and the bookstore grew rumored to be enchanted, cursed even.

Padraig walked through history books, then fantasy books, then books about gardening and food.

He arrived in the poetry section and found a skeleton on the floor. Its hair was all but gone, its clothes were shreds bugs crawling in and out and its hand pointed to writing in the dust.

"Nec laudas nisi mortuos poetas: tanti non est, ut placeam, perire" If only dead poets are praised I'd rather go unsung.

In the skeletons hand was a feather pen still filled with ink and beyond the writing in the shelves was an unfinished book. Padraig kneeled for a minute then moved on.

Beyond the poetry section he found a hag like woman, her hair was knotted and frayed. Her clothes were torn and dirty. The hag was barefoot, seemingly stuck to the spot she stood in. Just out of reach was a small trinket made of blue sapphire. Padraig picked it up and handed it to her. Instantly the ugly woman became beautiful. She looked at him for a minute.

"Thank you kind sir, but how will I ever leave the store without my shoes? I will be stuck here."

"Did you live in the village?"

"Yes my name is Elaganza Maranda."

"I will return for you with your shoes." Padraig had to hurry he did not know how long Mamie would last.

So he ran as fast as he could out of the store, mounted his horse, heels and all, valiantly riding back to the village.

"Do you know an Elaganza Maranda?" he said to the first woman he saw.

"Yes she went missing weeks ago, her shoes are still waiting for her by her front doorstep down by the café." The woman responded, so off Galloway rode.

He found the house along with the shoes, collected them and rode back to the bookstore. When he returned to Elaganza he helped her put her shoes on.

"Miss I must ask why did you come to this store?"

"I was in my garden one day looking at my trinket when I saw a strange stone I touched it and felt it wished to be returned. When I got to the book store entrance, well that is all I seem to remember. I do remember there was a strict no shirt, no shoes, no service policy."

"Thank you. I will lead you out and then I must find another damsel." So Padraig led Elaganza out of the store. He helped her through the weeds and saw her off on her way.

Once Elaganza had walk off towards town he returned to the store.

He worked his way through children's books, then books about gladiators, after that came auto and plain old biographies and finally music where he found another sign that read.

"Aude sapere." Dare to know.

"Galloway would know what all these signs meant where is he when I need him?" Padraig said aloud.

The next aisle over he found Mamie very lightly transformed. She fortunately had not been in the bookstore long. Her hair was filled with spiders that were trying to weave their webs, while other bugs tried to eat at her green dress.

She was in a section of books all about the human body and the wonderful things inside of it. One of her hands with its painted fingertips was reaching out, while the other clutched a glowing rock over her heart.

Padraig walked over to look into her foggy eyes. He picked a book off the shelf with an emerald heart on the front. Padraig handed her the book with the emerald heart engraved on its front, and then placed her shoes on her feet. She blinked, then thought, breathed and finally snapped out of the stores curse. Mamie dropped the glowing rock, something was carved into it.

"Do you know what made you come here?"

"I was reading my book in my hammock, when I noticed this strange glowing rock, I touched it and felt it wanted me to return it. I remember walking barefoot all the way up the mountain road. Then there was nothing till now."

"That is alright, just one more question, what does *Credo elvem etiam vivere* mean?" Mamie had carved something out of the rock, Padraig could ask her what she had carved.

"Credo elvem etiam vivere, um," she muttered thinking "translated it means I believe Elvis lives."

"Who is Elvis?"

"I have no idea. Please get me out of this place." As Padraig led Mamie out of the store he noticed that the back of the entrance sign had a different saying then the front,

"Bene, cum Latine nescias, nolo manus meas in te maculare" He was happy he wouldn't have to try to read the signs anymore, Mamie translated it for him.

"Well, if you don't understand plain Latin, I'm not going to dirty my hands on you" she said.

"I cannot walk you home I am sorry for that, I must return to make sure no person ever gets stuck in there again."

"The book store was a wonderful place once, will you return it to its former glory?" Mamie asked smiling.

"I'll do what I can" Padraig took what he heard to heart and heels still on, he watched Mamie walk off then once and for all walked back into the store.

"Plain Latin," he said to himself.

As he journeyed through the isles he noticed more and more of the books he had rushed by trying to save Mamie as fast as possible. The newest books were all written in English. He went searching for the oldest books he could find based off of a strange hunch he had. Padraig could tell by the dust on the books he was getting closer and closer, when finally he saw a figure in a brown moldy cloak, hood pulled up around the back of their head, slowly shuffling.

"How are you moving about down here" Padraig thought to himself "Mamie and Elaganza were stuck." He snuck up behind the figure as gently and quietly as he could. Not knowing it knew he had been there since he entered the store.

"Sir Knight do not dare touch my hood, if you mess up a single hair on my head I will have you dead in the blink of a heavily lashed eye."

"Are you the one who keeps bringing these poor women and girls here?"

"Not I." said the figure. "The store itself has summoned them and will keep bringing them until they learn their lesson. Reading is fundamental. Knowledge should come before material possessions. Most of all never leave home without your shoes. Until they figure those three essentials then the enchantment of this store will keep drawing them in like moths to the spotlight."

"Maybe if you didn't shun them for being who they are instead of who you want them to be they would come to visit you again, you cannot just go forcing people into doing things." Padraig said.

The figure finally turned around, she was the second most beautiful person he had ever seen. Her hair was amber colored in ringlets, her face seemed painted on like a china doll not a single line slightly out of place. When she spoke again he was stunned at how lifeless she was. She was cold as ice in her mannerisms.

"And how would one go about doing that sir winning them over by sweeping in and saving the day?"

"No, by being a caring listening person, I heard the women of this town used to come here often but grew scared of it why is that?"

"I took it over and I am better than all of them."

"You are no better than anyone else, if there is one thing I know for sure it is that we are all equal. We are all human."

"I am sorry but I lost my humanity somewhere when I took over, isolated, alone in a dark dusty place like this you would too."

"Your... you lost your shoes..."

"My shoes, honey I'm too amazing to need shoes, look at these amazing feet I have." And she was right she did have amazing feet but, this store as he had read had a no shoes, no shirt, no service curse protecting it. He sat down and removed the heels, not letting his feet touch the ground.

"Try these on for size, they are as beautiful as you are and I do not deserve to wear them." He said as fast as he could. She pitied him for a minute and slipped her pristine foot into one of the shoes. It fit like a glove.

"I need the other shoe as well Sir, just one does not make an outfit." She said a bit more warm. So Padraig put the other shoe on her foot. She stood for a minute, blinked and sighed.

"I am so sorry Sir I must have lost my footing when I lost my shoes."

"It is fine," instead of standing on his feet he jumped up on both hands and balanced himself.

"Just one thing, Ma'am."

"Rita Layworthy is the name."

"Miss Layworthy, you need to make a sign in every language that says no shoes, no shirt, no service. Not everyone understands Latin." He laughed and walked on his hands out of the store, where he put on his own boots got back on his horse and rode into town.

Demona, Ruby Lu and Mamie were waiting in the yard. They cheered as he rode up and dismounted. Mamie ran up and gave Padraig a big hug and kissed him on the cheek.

"She seems so much more caring then she did when she was wandering off, but we could not stop her, she kept screaming in Latin and ripping her heels off of her feet." said Ruby Lu.

"Thank you Sir Padraig." All three of the women said at once. For the first time in Padraig's life the solution was not one of strength but one of cleverness and thought.

"Since I don't need this anymore why don't you give this book of poems to someone close to you Sir Padraig? They might be able to find a poem that makes them think of you." Mamie said as she handed Padraig the book. Padraig flipped through the pages fast, he was not much of a reader, but one poem caught his eye. He felt it might help Galloway understand him. So he got on his horse and rode home.

As he rode up to the Hughes house Galloway saw him and ran up to greet him. Padraig reached into his satchel for the book his hand was on it when Galloway spoke.

"Your mother…"

"What about her?" And he instantly forgot all about the book.

While Padraig was away his mother had been thrown off a horse and she was not doing well. He rushed to her side.

As he entered the room he saw his father, Sir Warburton on one side of the bed. His mother lay in bed she was visibly broken, Padraig almost broke then and there but he knew he had to be strong for her.

"I waited for your return." She said as she looked at him with her caring brown eyes. Padraig kneeled down at her side.

"What did you find my brave son?"

"I found something for Galloway."

"Is it enough for you as well?"

"I don't know."

"I am glad you found something for him, but I asked if you found something for yourself." She smiled fading away.

41

"I haven't."

"Keep looking…" were the last words to leave her lips.

Lady Jane Kenly's funeral was held two days later. The day was rainy when they put her in the ground, beneath her favorite field of flowers. A small statue was placed above the place she rested. It depicted the young woman she once was before she was a mother or a wife. Lady Jane and her mother had saved the women of Timbre Town from trolls by simply using their words. Plenty came to say their farewells to the woman, calling her an angel. Padraig did not talk to anyone. For days after, he roamed the farms. When he could not roam anymore he got on his horse, High Chance, and rode till High Chance would not move. When Galloway tried to talk to Padraig, Padraig simply refused to listen. Not even Sir Warburton could get through to him. One day Padraig mounted High Chance and galloped off unsure if he would ever return.

Sir Padraig Kenly rode the horse to Kohln, he rode High Chance it to Timber Town, but neither beast nor man found peace there. The women that had known of his loss offered him comfort through food, but a full stomach did not fix his emptiness. Padraig and High Chance rode to the far south western shore. When a ship's captain asked if Padraig, looking like a good strong man to lift and haul cargo, as well as assist in protecting the ship would join Padraig agreed. That day Padraig set High Chance free to roam a wild apple orchard, likely never to meet again.

Padraig sailed to the shore of Barcales, where he had vanquished vampires He sailed to Ong Ala Con, the most advanced fortress and earned a new name, The Silent White Knight. His strength and skill helped him to lift boulders when an earthquake hit collapsing parts of the underground tunnels. Padraig could not stop, he would not rest. His mind was filled with one thought that he was fighting in a way he was not used to. Padraig stayed with this ship through the rough seas around the south coast of Jara. Beyond the Wia Islands and passed Nesia, farther than the Pass of High Stones nothing was far enough, not even halfway around the world. If he would have been honest with himself he would have figured out he didn't even know what he was looking for.

One day the ship took him to the island of Manula in the southern seas, where a revolution was being fought. Magic had started here along with time itself. Its natives had embraced magic but never let its power rule them. After a long history of other lands trying to abuse the power, a group had risen up. This group called itself the Pack. They believed if they sent away those who could perform magic then other lands would leave them alone. So those who could use its powers left for the love of their families. Once freedom was gained it was also lost. Most natives decided they would rather have their loved ones back. The Pack grew unpleasant ruling each island through fear and oppression. As the ship docked it was clear to Padraig the people were holding something back. As night fell the ship's crew settled itself down in a small tavern. The natives sung songs loudly in rounds, they sang of a fight that was burning deep within them. Padraig stood at the back of the room and listened as a man approached him slowly.

"Your shield, it is the symbol of a man who has many legends surrounding him." The stranger spoke a white hooded cloak pulled over his eyes. His almost purple lips spoke words in a broken manner. Padraig nodded.

"They call you the Silent White Knight. You come from the Kingdom of Rue," the man said. "I seek a man like you to help."

"Help with?" Padraig said using as few words as possible.

"You do speak."

"It is a secret."

"Secrets…" The man started and Padraig raised his finger pressing it against the man's lips. "Sorry, we cannot be free here. Join us, help us. We just want to be with our loved ones again but the Pack keeps us apart. If they know we are close they move our loved ones."

"I will help."

"We meet down the way at the abandoned temple. Two bells from now," the man said and left Padraig's side. Padraig did as he was told. He waited for the clock to chime two times, then he made his way down to the temple where men waited for him. A revolt happened that night with the Silent White Night at its front line. When the sun came up, the ship sailed but Padraig stayed.

After a few weeks of helping the natives fight for freedom, people began to question why he was there, it would always be summed up in a simple conversation.

"He does not look like us…" a voice chimed up.

"He is fighting on our side and he is good at it are you going to complain?"

"No," the islander patted Padraig's back, "Welcome brother."

Padraig fought without a single word for so long that most thought he was mute with the exception of the one man that had asked him for his help on his first night in Manula.

Padraig stood on the edge of a jungle where a major victory had just been claimed. The lone knight looked out at the ocean, the sand gray beneath his metal boots. The other man approached him.

"You seek something here," the other man said. Padraig did not look back at the stranger.

"I seek justice."

"It is more than that."

"I knew someone who loved a wizard. So I am here to find him."

"That is almost a lie," the stranger said.

"Why do you fight?" Padraig asked.

"My love was taken after I was exiled. I fight to find him. May I keep you company?"

"If you swear not to tell anyone I can speak, they ask too many questions of strangers."

"I swear a vow of silence from now until we both find who we seek," said the stranger from under his white hooded cloak.

The two of them stayed at the front of the revolution from Caborne to Ankalas to Maba and in every other major battle of the Southern Islands.

After a year, the revolution was almost won. One small Pack survived in a town called Pampanya. Padraig and his hooded companion arrived with their squadron of revolutionaries.

In a last ditch effort to keep a strong hold, the Pack was currently terrorizing as many houses as they could.

"Help, the Pack is here to take me again." A voice came from inside a small brick house that a few of the Pack seemed focused on. Padraig gallantly defeated each and every member, knocking the last one out Padraig helped the man they had attacked up. He was bruised and bleeding. His companion rushed in soon after for the first time he pulled the cloak off his head. The two men's eyes locked. The two lovers were finally reunited.

The man who had fought beside him looked Padraig in the eyes.

"Thank you." He bowed his head with its large brown eyes. He turned to the bruised man and held him. "Capit, my sweet Capit."

"Doon!" Capit said as they embraced each other, close to crying from pure joy.

"Doon?" Padraig said.

"I am sorry I did not tell you my name. I didn't think you wanted to know it."

"You are Galloway's wizard. Do you understand what you have made me lose?"

"What is wrong?" Doon responded half shocked. Padraig gripped Doon's cloaks and almost lifted him clear into the air. Without a word his face said everything it needed to. He then placed Doon back and stepped away.

"Galloway was sick, he almost died. Then I used magic and saved him, but the magic, I think it changed me, so I left for a while to clear my head. While I was gone I lost my mother. If you had never taught him magic this would have never happened" Padraig's voice was becoming desperate.

"He also would not be alive," Doon sighed. "You saved him."

Capit stepped between the two. He had similar deep brown eyes, and dark black hair, with a hint of caramel on his skin.

"Stop this now. Both of you, what is the real issue?"

"There is no issue, this brave knight and I have fought to find you. I was thanking him. Then I was going to tell him the fight was ours from here on out."

"I will be going then," Padraig said and turned away frustrated as his mind whirled. All this fighting had been beside the one man, Padraig wanted so strongly to hate. Padraig left the house using his legs to walk as fast as he could. Doon rushed after him.

"Wait Knight...how is Sir Galloway?" Doon asked. Padraig stopped dead in his tracks.

"He is healed now, of all except a wounded heart, I could not fix that, like I could not save my own mother. I have not seen him in almost a year now, I hope he has moved on."

"That is more of a lie than simply searching for me. I am sorry for your loss, we all have our fights and our struggles. I had to stay away for decades from my Capit, but an opportunity arose so I took it. Every day I see him will make that time we couldn't be together seem like a distant memory. There is only one magic to help a heart, time. Go back to Galloway tell him what you really feel."

"While he was sick he said your name. He said I could never grasp his secret."

"Have you figured out what it is?"

"I know what it is… I know it. How can I return it? This is not about being brave, this is not about defeating something I cannot vanquish it. I can't even see it."

"Exactly. He can help you. He has seen it since the day you saved a family from a fire. He has been thinking these thoughts for most of his life. He needs someone brave. You have come all this way, spent all this time knowing what he needs. It is something I could have never given him. Go." Doon said and sent Padraig off without another word.

When he returned to the wild apple orchard he found High Chance was living a horse's happily ever after. There was an orphanage on the other side of the orchard so children would come to pet him. Padraig was happy his horse had found what it was looking for so the knight went off on his way home.

The day Padraig arrived was the day before his eighteenth birthday. He left a letter on Galloway's tower caught within the vines. Along with the book of poems which Padraig had kept so he could reread one poem over and over.

"Meet me at the wishing well, I have returned. I do hope this gift will be enough for you to forgive me for my absence.~ Padraig"

That night they met at the wishing well. Galloway had grown to his full height. He was a foot or so taller than Padraig now. He had hair pulled back with the help of a silver diadem. He wore a poets black shirt and pants to match with simple leather boots. Padraig wore brown pants and a white shirt he usually saved for rare occasions at the palace.

Their eyes could not avoid each other's as hard as they seemed to try. For a while they stood looking at each other in silence. Both shifting awkwardly, attempting to speak first but both failing.

Padraig bearing his forearms showed off ink that had been pressed into his flesh on his adventures overseas. He did not want to brag to Galloway however what each one meant because suddenly they all meant little.

"I waited for you." Galloway said regretting how fast he spoke.

"I know."

"I read the book, I even found a favorite poem." Galloway said breaking the silence. "Line 87 by Henley Kurit…" Galloway removed the book from his bag and placed it on the edge of the well. Padraig waited breathing trying not to seem too eager. He then picked up the book and found the poem. It was the same poem that had caught Padraig's eye, the same poem Padraig had been reading every night for the last year.

Line Eighty Seven
By Henley Kurit

If what you seek is lost then hold.
Hold close.
Under sleep we find what we dream of most.

The moon is the sun's true love and they will
always fill in where the other cannot.

The water is earths
And fire's lover is the spark.

The moon is watching us and it bathes us in its white pale
light.

I take your hand in mine as you take my hand in
yours,
and the night sky makes us one.

The stars bless us. They are our gifts glistening for all human
kind to see.

We shall be married.

We shall be one, like the gods, the stars, the earth and the sun.

Never forgotten,

Our love has won.

After reading the passage Galloway gently closed the book. He placed it on the edge of the wishing well and looked at it. He remembered all those years ago when Padraig had told him the well was broken but he made a wish right then and there anyway. The same wish he had come to the well to make every night since Padraig had left.

"What was your wish all those years ago?" Galloway said once more breaking the silence.

"It doesn't matter...it never came true anyway." Padraig said.

"It does to me, you swore you'd tell me one day."

"I wished for someone who would love me more than I loved myself. I was being stupid."

"I was coming to disprove magic wishing wells." Galloway laughed. "What you wished for matters, I think it did come true." Galloway said rapidly.

Midnight struck, the bells could be heard from a faraway church. Both of the boys were eighteen now, Padraig had finally caught up to something Galloway had felt for a long time. The wishing well waited slightly echoing their words, so inaudibly they became the sound of dripping water.

"Do you know what I wish..." Galloway said.

"Wishes should be kept a secret." Padraig grinned in the moonlight. He was giving in finally.

"You may be right, they have more magic that way..." Galloway responded and the two had a moment they would hold as their secret.

A few years passed by as their lives continued on. Their fame as knights grew. Sir Padraig Kenly and Sir Galloway Hughes were known kingdom wide.

-

While listlessly riding around the kingdom they passed a tavern on the southern border. The two saw a man on a black horse riding away as fast as he could with a brown sack in hand. The tavern owner was running after him as fast as he could.

"Stop thief, stop." The owner bellowed. Off like lightning the two knights chased the man on the black horse down. He was no match for them. They forced him to dismount and bound his arms together. Galloway took the sack full of stolen goods and they walked back to the tavern. The tavern owner was a plump man, who wore brown robes much like a friar's garb. He had the haircut and a small thin beard to match.

"This is yours sir." Galloway said to the man who owned the tavern.

"Thank you kind Sir Galloway and Sir Padraig."

"He knows us Padg." Galloway said laughing.

"Of course who in the kingdom doesn't, come in, come in. Welcome to Tip Tavern."

"Are you Tip?"

"No, Tip was my father. I am Archibald Turpin."

They were led inside, they left the thief on a barstool as they were led to a booth. That night Turpin asked for their tale. So they told him of how they met by the well, they told him of how they were knighted, and in the end he had one question.

"What did you wish for at the well Sir Padraig?"

"It really doesn't matter to our story, not yet." The two knights smiled. The sun had risen outside so they took the thief to the king for his punishment.

Another month flew by, the knights along with their fathers were summoned to again do the bidding of the king. Yvonne at his side throwing fits no knights paid her any attention. He needed four men to stop the Elite from converting any more families into brainwashed slaves.

The knights suited up and headed out, across the tides of the Aribadell Sea to the fishing village of Wettinton.

When they arrived they were greeted by hordes of brainwashed villagers. The villagers shuffled their feet with arms hanging limp at their sides, their jaws hung ajar, mouths wide open moaning and groaning.

Up on the top of a hill on a precipice of a tower not watching the knights' actions was a figure in a diamond colored cloak.

"We will have to blend in." Galloway whispered. The knights' gave up their posture and shuffled right along, mouths open. Padraig even picked up on drooling.

The figure in the cloak must have caught a reflection of light off of the knight's armor because he looked at them and tilted his head like something was not quite right. He raised his hands their way with open palms and pulled them back toward himself over and over. So the knights pretended to obey him. They groaned and stumbled till they were almost right beneath him. He pulled back his hood to reveal his tattooed head.

"Bow before the Elite!" He hollered down. But Sir Padraig, Sir Warburton and Sir Caleb were too proud. Galloway began to bow, halting thanks to the feeling of looking quite foolish.

"What?" he bellowed, then screamed "OBEY ME!" the doors behind him burst open and there were three other cloaked figures who were now supremely distraught. They all pulled back their diamond colored hoods. All of them were tattooed on almost every inch of their skin. Two of them female, raised their arms first, then the men. There was silence. The moaning and groaning had stopped. As the knights looked around they realized each and every one of the brain washed villagers was now watching them.

"I have a feeling they don't like us knights" said Sir Padraig.

"Draw your swords men" said Sir Warburton.

"Most of them are women and children" said Galloway, so they drew their weapons and dropped them.

"No weapons shall be used today men." Caleb said with a heavy voice. Padraig and Sir Warburton, both gave each other a nod. They held up their shields and rushed towards the door. Sir Caleb and Galloway followed behind knocking the door down like a battering ram. The villager's rambled behind.

"Leave your shields as a door." Galloway said with a new bright idea. So they blocked up the entrance as best as they could. At the top of the tower the Elite cast down badly aimed spells. These four tattooed magicians were simply not enough and the knights knew it. So the knights avoided their spells dodging and weaving to climb up the stairs.

The villager's burst through their shields and followed a bit faster than before. The knights tackled down three of the Elite and tied them up while the other tried pelting them with magical knives. They bounced right off shattering easily.

A bright beam of light broke through the clouds bouncing off of armor and cloaks. Blinding Galloway for a brief second he could swear he saw an angel. There was this beautiful person, the most amazing sight Galloway had ever seen right in front of his eyes and all he could do was stare thoughtless. Galloway breathed and twisted his head, there was his father in grave danger. A group of brainwashed mothers was about to push Sir Caleb off the precipice, he refused to strike at them.

In came Padraig, he picked up the mothers, pulling them away from Sir Caleb barely saving his life. While Sir Warburton gave the final member of the Elite a good clonk on the head. After which the villagers became free. The four knights took the Elite back to the King for proper punishment.

On the way home Tip Tavern called their name. Before going in the two knights waited and watched as the sun set. Their horses, Olive and Chase, stood as close as two pages in a book. The first star appeared in the evening sky. The two knights gave each a quick glance, their hands clasped around each other's for a moment. They both grinned like they used to as young boys, then blinked and let out all the words they needed to with just a breath. They dismounted their horses and went inside.

"Back so soon?" Turpin asked when he saw them at the bar.

"On our way home, we needed a place to keep our horses and lay our heads. We figured a drink and a meal wouldn't be such a bad thing either. Why not top it off with a friend" Padraig said.

"He always knows what to say? At just the right moment" Turpin asked Galloway.

"You hit the nail on the head."

"I cannot offer you drinks on the house tonight friends." Turpin sighed. "Unless," His voice cheered up. "You share with me another one of your tales, how about a loved one of either of yours that you may have found on your voyages." The knights looked at each other briefly.

"I think I've got tonight's story covered Padg, if you don't mind that is?" said Galloway.

"Go for it, I don't think I've ever heard you spin a tale" responded Padraig. Galloway told the story of their most recent adventure.

"Luckily now the boars have come back and the families of Wettinton are no longer brainwashed." Galloway capped off his story. The three men laughed together and drank until they could barely stand.

"What of the angel, the most beautiful person, Sir Galloway?"

"Like Padg's wish it really doesn't matter" Galloway laughed and before Turpin asked more Padraig cut in.

"We forgot to ask if you have a room to spare Sir Archibald Turpin." Padraig said bowing.

"Yes but only one bed in the room, you two being knights should be used to such small quarters I'm sure. You must share tents and such on all your adventures."

"Yes one bed shall be fine my friend."

"It is up the stairs first door on the left, good night brave and valiant heroes. May you dream of the wild boars!" Turpin stood and raised his empty mug. Padraig assisted Galloway up the stairs and into bed where they instantly passed out.

As they rode the next morning they came to find the royal carriage was stopped in the middle of the road. Princess Yvonne stormed out in a rage, she was screaming and bickering at the top of her voice when a familiar frigid air swooped by.

The icy air picked her up and began to carry her fast. Galloway and Padraig lay chase. Down the glen across the fields, deep into the woods they chased her and the wind. The wind took her straight down along a river. Finally she vanished midair with the sound of a wooden door slamming shut. The knights halted, dismounting from their horses.

"I see no door Gall."

"I bet it is there however." Galloway said and the two trudged into the river arms out feeling for something physical, and there they felt it, a door handle they could not see. They opened the door and could see a long hallway. So in the two went, the door slamming behind them. Paintings of women lined the walls, they all had such sullen faces on.

"Where are we?" Padraig asked.

The cold rush returned to sweep around them then stand in front of them somehow suddenly visible.

The wind became a faceless figure of ice that began to shift and change taking many shapes from their past until it picked one. When its form was complete another Galloway stood before them. He was sickly looking and dark, his skin covered in frost.

"The palace of empty hearts." The dark Galloway said. "When your ruler, La Rue, was young he came here and saved his loved one, the princess's mother. Like kings before him and kings before them. He filled her heart with love and when she was lost in childbirth the castle needed to find a new heart. That would be the princess's. It could only take her once, I, the cold wind could invade her heart completely. Find the princess and you may keep her but only if she does not say a single word within these walls."

The dark Galloway led them deeper inside, beyond another door way waited a maze of corridors all lined with mirrors.

Behind each mirror sat a different Yvonne, some of them were noticeably off with green hair or buttons for eyes while others the only difference would be the item in their hand.

"She can still be saved. Her glass," he tapped a mirror to his side the child behind it threw a silent tantrum swinging a wooden sword to no avail. "...has not yet been solidified. If she should make a noise, even the smallest of peeps, sealed forever she will be. Good luck young knights." The dark Galloway paced.

"No say of which glass she's behind, why do these quests always have to have a challenge?" Sir Padraig asked.

"If there was no challenge anyone could complete them." Sir Galloway responded "I have a guess at how to solve this one, as always." He grinned. He approached a mirror, putting his hand on the cold hard glass. The sharp toothed Yvonne behind frowned as hard as it could, squeezing its teddy bear as its face turned purple red. There was his idea, the glint in his eye. Padraig could see it.

"Padg, touch every mirror you can."

"If she hears us she will scream and fuss Gall."

"Off with our armor then." So they stripped down to their soft fabric clothes. Both started touching various mirrors as gently as they could.

Finally they were left to four mirrors, all of them looking identical to Yvonne, one with a locket. Another held a ball of yarn. One with a hairbrush on a nightstand, her room was there but fading and the last read out of an old leather book. Sir Galloway pointed

60

to the girl whose room was still there, she did not face them as her brush was behind her. Galloway recognized the hairbrush it was her mothers.

He pressed his finger to his lips miming to sneak up it was almost like a dance. Sir Padraig could be soft and gentle if Sir Galloway showed him how to do it right for the time and place. Padraig quickly took off a sock and readied himself. He went first through the jelly like glass. Wrapping his hand, with the sock around to her mouth, and his other arm around her chest, he picked her up. Instantly Galloway snatched up the hairbrush. Mouthing as best he could,

"Stay quiet or we leave this behind." Yvonne nodded. Sir Padraig carried her into the hallway.

"We are going to let you go if you scream we push you back in, and then you end up like these other kids." They showed her the other mirrors, she nodded. Galloway gave her a halfhearted grin. Padraig placed her down removing the sock.

"Mine." She said simply, pointing at her hairbrush. As the end of the word left the tip of her tongue her mirror shattered. Screams of the other Yvonne's started to hum breaking into the silence. The dark Galloway was there in the blink of an eye.

"I told you let her make no sound what did you not understand about that?" The dark Galloway said.

"She shall become the coldest soul in all the lands..." The dark Galloway bellowed as it chased them, slowly losing its shape and form, it was turning back into the wind again.

"Let's get out of here Gall, my head hurts from the noise."

"Follow us fast and you'll get this back," Galloway waved the brush. "Don't and well you might not find your way out."

The screams grew louder as more glass broke flying to and fro, cutting their skin and clipping their hair. She knew his words were true. So she followed them, they ran down the hall till they found the entrance. They slammed the door to the halls behind them running for the main door as fast as their legs could carry them. The two knights were slightly in front of Yvonne as they opened the door to the outside world. The young knights' lept, when Yvonne went to leap out the wind snatched her by her ankle. Padraig and Galloway each grabbed a wrist and pulled. They won the fight and the wind was gone. Her ankle had an ice cold hand print on it that began to spread.

As they helped Yvonne onto the back of Padraig's horse they whispered to each other.

"We need to change her heart, the wind will be inside of it in no time and then we will have failed..." Galloway said and Padraig agreed, when suddenly Galloway had a plan. "Change the mind, change the heart?"

"Little bruise to the ego usually does the trick." Padraig said smiling. They rode off to the wishing well as fast as possible.

When they arrived at the old wishing well the sun was beginning to set. They had to rush if they wished to return the princess to King Rue.

"Would you like to make a wish princess?"

She looked at them, they could see the ice on the skin of her hand.

"Simply lower your brush down in the well and wish away." They said at once and as she leaned over they pushed her in.

A burst of cold air shot up and out of the well passing by the knights faces sweeping back their hair.

"Ouch" said Yvonne.

The icy wind saw a new pair of victims' two young men with more fear inside of them than anyone it had known before. The knights helped Yvonne out of the well and onto her horse where she sat quite content. Her skin was pink and healthy.

Off the three galloped.

In no time they arrived at King Charlatte La Rue's castle. They escorted the princess inside. All the men they passed bowed trembling in fear. One still was missing all his hair. The last time he had seen her she ripped it out, follicle by follicle. This time she just smiled and blinked walking daintily as she could.

Into the king's dining hall. He had recently finished his mashed nuts and blueberry mush sandwich. His jaw dropped and he stood staring at Yvonne.

"Here you go your Eminence, your daughter renewed, if you don't mind the slight bump on her head." Padraig said part of it under his breath.

"She gave it to herself. It was the last tantrum she will ever throw. The last time she'll be beast, the finale to your woe" said Galloway.

"Unlike before only time shall tell young Knights if she has had the last scream. I am sad to say I cannot give you any glory until I am sure. Return to me after three full moons and I can then give you my praise." The King said as he pulled out a chair for his daughter to sit. Yvonne sat down properly then pulled in her seat. She drank tea and ate crumpets, only responding when talked to. She lifted her pinky when she lifted her cup.

The knights smiled and allowed the king some much needed bonding time with his now unspoiled child.

They stopped into Turpin's Tavern and told him of the tale so far.

They took their time going home to the farms by the well. Passed the onions and cabbages, they passed the servants' huts as well.

"Whenever I return home Gall, I feel like I might as well be dead."

"I know what you mean Padg. But we are close to another adventure I can smell it in the air."

"That I believe old friend is manure you smell. I fear for the day we become our fathers' ages and we no longer have the energy to wander the lands."

"Then Padg, let us make sure that while we are young we do as much as we can." Galloway began to think on the many spells Doon once talked of. He had something to get done without Padraig's knowledge.

"See you in a few days' time Galloway. Maybe we will find an adventure to fill in those long three full moons."

"See you soon Padg." Galloway strode off on his brown spotted horse. Padraig went his own way.

Their fathers' who had been promoted to counselors of the king greeted them and asked of all that they had seen. Lady Claudia made them the most filling meals. They washed up, dried off and went straight to bed.

A few days passed by and as much as the knights could they stayed off their feet. But restless as always Padraig needed another adventure to complete.

So he mounted his horse clad in armor once more and rode to see Galloway. Galloway was up in his tower reading away. He had found a scroll on what the moving clouds Doon had left carved on his shield meant. They would let him travel once in his sleep without his physical body ever moving. Galloway was now just waiting on the perfect night. His many inventions surrounded him, his gadgets and weapons, on the walls were all his drawings of contraptions with wings.

"Sir Galloway Hughes, come down let me in" cried out Padraig. Galloway leaned out the window so high off the ground.

"Who are you, your hair has grown long?" Galloway mocked. Padraig reached up with one hand and ruffled his long black hair. His hair had grown quite long on their journey to save the princess. It was starting to curl.

"Come cut it for me and save me from these wretched curls that you seem to despise so much."

"Me! You are the one who begs for a close blade to swiftly cut them away, what every new moon?"

"I deny it, now hurry up and let me in so you may be done with them oh clever Sir Galloway Hughes."

"Why not use your own arms and climb, strongest in the land Sir Padraig Kenly?" he responded looking down.

"I have recently bathed and would rather save my strength for our next outing. Please let me in."

"Fine, give me a moment" Galloway said with a grin. Galloway had sealed up the door a long time ago to make sure that his valuable ideas would stay safe out of view. He had studied many things that he wished to keep. He would only use them if he must or if Padraig had begged.

So Galloway switched on a crank that kicked up a switch, leading down many gears clicking and grinding till in front of Sir Padraig the ground opened up. He went underground, the secret door sealing itself above his head, then straight through the tunnel and right up the stairs. Padraig knew not to ask how Galloway ever got in.

Galloway gave Padraig a close cut, freeing his thick skull from its dark hair. Galloway left barely an inch, just as they both liked it.

They spent most of the next three weeks like they used to as kids. They worked with their horses and lived their small lives. Waiting and wanting to be together one night. They both knew what had happened over the many years. They grew together and cured each other's small fears. They filled in the blanks where the other one lacked.

On the night before Padraig and Galloway returned to King Charlatte La Rue, neither slept in his bed. They went to Galloway's tower to make a pact. Padraig noticed Galloway's glimmering shield but dared not ask.

"What will we ask the king this time Padg?"

"This time we will ask to become family Gall. We have reunited his. So I think it is time that we ask to join our lives."

"And what if he refuses?"

"Then we will go somewhere far far away that they'd never expect, to live out our lives. We can adventure elsewhere, we can find other kings. Where we can be in love, we will take love as our gift." Sir Padraig Kenly said as Sir Galloway Hughes fell asleep with Padraig's chest under his head, his last movement was to touch the shield with the back of his hand.

In the land of dreams Sir Galloway stood, he had to go and seek out his old friend one last time. He flew through the clouds over the oceans, half a world away, to find Doon. He arrived on the Southern Islands and searched them, coming upon a young man with Doon's clouds tattooed across his arms. Capit's tattoos shifted and drifted in the same magical manner. He lifted his head and Galloway felt as if he knew him. But the young man could not see him. From up in a window Galloway saw movement. He walked through the door and found Doon there scribing away. Moving maps of the tower on the wall. Paintings of Galloway's life as if Doon had been there all along. Watching him, protecting him. Telulla squawked in her cage.

"Hello there Galloway." Doon said without turning to face him. Galloway knew Doon would know, hearing his voice sparked up so many different feelings.

"Is that him? Is that Capit?"

"Yes, we have been in love for ages, my people live much longer than yours do. Magic is in our blood but it only shows in a few." In that instant Galloway moved on. He had loved someone for as long as he could as well, but he just hadn't come to fully let that sink in, he had his walls up.

"I see you used the shield."

"I waited as long as I could."

"I know." Doon said.

"Have you been watching over me this whole time?" Galloway said looking around the room.

"Well Telulla gets bored easily so I let her fly around and she kept going back to the tower."

"I see." Galloway went over to Telulla and pet her gently.

"You are afraid of losing Padraig?"

"I am, the wind took my shape in the palace of empty hearts. I am afraid to let him fully in Doon. If I do let him in though what if he runs away."

"Remember this, an empty heart feeds on fear. You are still afraid to love him, which is why it chose your shape. When you cannot think he will do it for you and in turn you will be brave when he is trembling. Go Gall, it is time for you to wake up." Doon said and Galloway did as he was told. He awoke to the sunlight his head still upon Padraig's chest. He chose to close his eyes again so that Padraig could wake him.

In the morning they bathed, mounted and rode to the king to claim the one thing that they lacked. They arrived before lunch and the king's men all cheered. The cure did the trick the princess was fine, she hadn't gone off in even the slightest of tiffs. Finally the king asked them,

"Now young Knights, how may I repay you, you may ask for anything, and it shall instantly be yours."

"We wish to be..." Padraig said.

"Married." Galloway finished his sentence. The two kneeled in front of the King bowing their heads. No risk had ever come close to this one for the two knights. King Rue stood silently lips sealed. The king thought back on his own life as these two young men kneeled before him, He had seen them growing into men, he had given them challenges and struggles to overcome. He was so proud of them he considered them family. The doors and windows creaked open taking advantage of the silence. The frigid air trickled in surrounding the king it held him tight not letting him say anything.

The other knight's in the room bowed their heads not sure of what else to do. Yvonne 's jaw dropped as she stared.

The icy cold grip shook King Rue's head. It made him give a disapproving grin. They could not and would not question the king. The two stood, hand grasping hand and turned around and walked away from King Rue. They dropped their shields, there would be no blow more wounding than this one. They dropped their swords for nothing could be fought. They left behind armor as they walked out of the castle. Abandoning their horses they slowly walked together neither one saying a word.

They found their way back to Tip's Tavern.

"The Knights have returned once again. No princess on hand, is she well now? You look different lads, what has happened?" Turpin said as they walked into the Tavern.

"She is doing quite well it has been three weeks since we saved her from her spell." Padraig said.

"Before we get to telling of our quest however we want to ask, Turpin tell us a story of your youthful past." Galloway said hoping for something truly inspiring.

"Me, oh well then I must tell you of my time in the cities of sand." Turpin began his tale.

Beyond our lands south most boarders through Lungi's Pass I was sent in my youth. I must have been close to your age, oh the years that have passed. King Charlatte's father ruled then, King Ithaca Rue. He was the one who freed us from the gods of anger and wrath. And me, I was in his army as a Priest. Can you boys imagine that? Before my lips ever tasted drink I had a thing for faith.

Ithaca's greatest foe the, Bishop of Spite, Warren Von Ike was raising an army. He sent up a messenger who carried his angry god's symbol, and spoke only in tongues. So Ithaca sent us in return. We were to take down the Bishop and topple his god as peacefully as we possibly could. Ithaca's knights were my escorts and I was meant to be the key. I'd bless them and tell them that being happy was alright.

When we arrived in the cities of sands we worked from Tittua to Umher to Unkrand. City by city things seemed to be going alright no guards at the temples no fights in the streets we started to wonder if the things we had heard were correct. When I spoke in their houses they nodded their heads, any god by them would be a delight.

Finally we ran into a slight complication. The men at one temple simply refused to listen. So we went to a close tavern to plot out a plan. And guess what was there waiting, the very same men. They were seated at the bar their hands clasped in prayer when like lighting an idea struck my head.

"Drinks on the house" I hollered as we walked in, patting each man on one shoulder. "Since you put up with our ideas and you let us rest our heads." Once they got drinking we began to converse.

"We pray so that our god is not angry, we beg him not to send down his curse, we hope that he is pleased and doesn't make our lives worse."

"Why would a god do such a thing?" I asked at them with no clue.

"It is not our god directly, but our god speaks to Bishop Von Ike." They all said and spat.

"He's not a god though he's simply a man. It might just be that he does not understand." I told them how our god gave us life and ways we could live but left it to us for the things that we did. It took some more conversation but the ideas we shared started to sink in. They joined up with our crew in the morning and helped the word spread.

Five cities later guess who we found preaching of anger and wrath unlike ever before, the Bishop of Spite, we spat even thinking of what he was about. It was easy to do and caught on between us quite fast. It was almost a game with all that we passed. If his name had been mentioned or thought of at all, all in the room would spit on the floor.

He withdrew his sword pointing it right at my chest. So I walked up very boldly and let its point rest against my flesh.

"If you should kill me, will your god be satisfied or will he simply keep asking for death until all life has been wiped from the earth." I said.

"If I do not I fear my god will smite me on the spot along with all my people."

"Thus far I have heard of only you who smite your own men, no hand of god."

"What does your god have in hand for me?"

"I believe god gave life, other than that it is up to man himself."

"They call you a Priest, what kind of Priest says things like that?"

"A Priest that believes in mankind" I replied, he dropped his sword right there and for him his angry god died.

His people no longer feared of the punishment to come unless by their own hand did they do some kind of wrong.

And what you may wonder of Bishop Von Ike, well he lives down the lane with seven children and a wife. Once he found drinking would calm down his soul he used that to relax. His god of anger no longer took a toll. It no longer taxed him or riled up his mind. His blood doesn't boil it simply just pumps through his veins.

Turpin finished his tale and followed it up by saying.

"Now please my friends tell me of your most recent adventure in life."

It took them an hour and they both shared the tale up till the ending, close to the well. Galloway took over to finish it up while Padraig smiled and raised his cup.

"So we took her to the well where we first met to make a wish. We convinced her that if she dropped her mother's hairbrush into the bucket and lowered it down, she would get her wish, so she did. And when she leaned over to whisper, we knew what had to be done. For nothing can break an ego like a good fall" said Sir Galloway.

"What did she wish for?" Asked Turpin "We don't know but she seemed to be a lot better when we got her back out, a little wet but she hasn't thrown a tantrum since" said Sir Galloway.

"My wish however," said Sir Padraig "was very similar to my first, to be with Galloway for the rest of my life."

"I thought your first wish didn't matter?"

"It didn't then and there, but as we grew and became more than friends it mattered a lot. I learned I loved Sir Galloway and it was he that I wished for, someone to be in love with me more than I was with myself. Now my wish matters more than ever because the king could not help. He gave us no blessing. That's all that we asked."

"You asked to be married?" He asked, and they nodded, "I don't think I can help you either." They both stared at him scared. "It is up to each person what life they take. No god or other man may make such a decision. It is my guess that the angel you saw," Turpin said to Galloway "was none other than Padraig

75

himself, your knight in shining armor. It is also my guess that if Padraig should tell me of his loves that every single one of them would reside in you Sir Galloway."

"You no longer need to call us sir, we are no longer knights, and our armor is left behind. We have become a disgrace. We are sorry to come to you for this Turpin but what we ask from you is not marriage, it is for an escape."

"Like what poison? What fools are men that take their lives! Do you wish to run, and take the chance of being torn apart by distance from all that you know? You are knights if you choose to be, no king can decide that. You are also married if you choose to be."

"My thoughts are all gone, my cleverness vanished" said Galloway.

"And my courage it trembles like a leaf in the wind" said Padraig.

As Turpin was about to try and comfort them the icy gust burst the windows blowing the candles out, it forced Turpin to disapprove. The knights left the pub more broken than before.

They passed their own farms thinking that no good would be there, just the coldness of hearts and a void they could not bear. The two came to the wishing well.

Padraig leaned on the wishing well wall almost collapsing as tears started streaming down his face. Galloway had never seen him cry. The two sat backs against the wishing well. Galloway holding Padraig close.

"It ends where it began Gall. The whole kingdom will know about us. Even Turpin has denied us assistance." Said Padraig. Galloway did not know what to say, he stood there unknowing of what else would come their way.

"No more adventures my love" said Padraig.

"We have saved all and lost ourselves. What shall we do now? Turpin was right, going to some other land will bring us nothing but farther apart. And death would leave us nowhere better. We have done nothing but curse ourselves." Padraig said breathing heavily. Galloway's mind went swirling into a spiral, it drifted to the last time he saw his friend the wizard. He remembered Doon's words,

"When you cannot think he will do it for you and in turn you will be brave when he is trembling."

"We become brave one last time." Galloway said with a certain gusto that came from the depths of his soul. Padraig looked up at him utterly surprised.

"We demand that we are married. We demand that we are united as one. If they say that we are not we tell them it is not up to them that the deed is already done." He took Padraig's hand, pulling him up. "And if they should try to pull us apart we will know that no matter what, we are together in our hearts, Sir Padraig Hughes." When Galloway said this Padraig couldn't help but grin.

"The moon is watching us and it bathes us in its white pale light. Line Eighty Seven, Henley Kurit."

Padraig said a bit under his breath, it was Galloway's favorite line from his favorite book.

"I take your hand in mine as you take my hand in yours, and the night sky makes us one. The stars bless us, they are our gifts glistening for all human kind to see." He continued to recite. "We shall be married. We shall be one, like the gods, the stars, the earth and the sun." Padraig kissed Galloway,

"Sir Galloway Kenly." Galloway kissed back.

"With this wish I thee wed" said one.

"With this wish I thee wed" said the other.

The cold wind rushed at them from the deepness of the night as it had rushed at the King, and as it had rushed at Turpin. However the cold wind could not get to them, because their hearts had both been filled. The wind rushed right down the wishing well and was stuck. No one would help it out. No one would come along and raise it up in a bucket.

When the morning came they told their families, who welcomed them with open arms. Sir Warburton started off by simply shaking their hands but he could not hold in how joyous he was so he embraced the newlyweds squeezing them tight in his strong arms. Lady Claudia and Sir Caleb rejoiced by dancing around their kitchen and out into the yard.

"You will need a place to live." Lady Claudia said as she was swung around by her husband, beckoning the young men join in.

"The Wizards Tower has been unlived in for quite some time..." Sir Caleb offered. It was decided then and there where the lovers would set up their house.

They rode to see King Rue and proclaimed they had been wed by the moon herself. King Rue smiled and his entire court cheered for the heroes.

A festival was held for the newlyweds. People from all over came to see them, Maime and her sisters, Doon and Capit, some of the villagers from Koln and even Wettinton. A moment of silence that night was held for all of those who had lost themselves to the coldness in their own hearts. After that one was held for Padraig's mother, if it hadn't been for her their love might have never come to be as strong as it could be.

The two soon moved into Galloway's tower, which they would, over time, build a small bastion around.

As they grew older they found themselves raising five children that had all been expelled from other lands.

Their adventures continued far and wide, together. As time went on Sir Galloway Kenly and Sir Padraig Hughes became legend, which as always leads into becoming myth and one day as most heroes become, they turned into fairytales. Sometimes a fairytale can get forgotten, but as long as there is a person to tell it and a person to listen this one shall never be one of those fairytales.

The End.

Made in the USA
Middletown, DE
25 January 2017